the *Juggler*

written by

Celia Barker Lottridge

from a film by

Ariadne Ochrymovych

Screenplay by Michael Glassbourg

Still photography by Arne Glassbourg

North Winds Press

A Division of Scholastic-TAB Publications Ltd., Richmond Hill, Ontario, Canada

for Maria, Leo and Don

A.O.

for Andrew

C.B.L.

Canadian Cataloguing in Publication Data

Lottridge, Celia Barker.
  The juggler

ISBN 0-590-71519-4 (bound) - ISBN 0-590-71520-8 (pbk.)

I. Ochrymovych, Ariadne.   II. Title.

PS8573.087J83 1985   jC813'.54   C85-098477-7
PZ7.L67Ju 1985

1st printing 1985   **Printed in Hong Kong**

Barnaby opened the door of the stable and stepped out into bright sunshine. He grinned. It was a perfect day for his show. His drum and accordion hung round his neck, and over his shoulder he had slung a bag stuffed with his puppets and juggling balls. All he needed now was a crowd to watch him, and he was sure to find that in the marketplace.

On such a fine fall day, the people of Quebec City would be gathered there to buy food for the winter and to look over the latest goods that had arrived from Europe by sailing ship. With any luck, they would have money in their pockets and a holiday mood in their hearts. They should be ready for a good show, thought Barnaby. Performing for a cheerful crowd was the best fun he knew.

He decided to take the long way to the marketplace. If he played his accordion as he went, a few children were sure to follow him, and they would help attract a crowd to watch his juggling and his tricks.

Down the narrow, crooked streets he made his way, playing a lively tune. People looked out of doorways and windows and waved to him as he went past. Soon there were six or seven children marching in a straggling line behind him. One took the drum, and the others picked up sticks and beat time on the stone walls of the houses as they passed.

"Hey, Barnaby," called one of the children, "we aren't going down the Rue des Jardins, are we? Those rich people might not like us."

"Don't be silly," said Barnaby, turning around to show off his patched pants and ragged jacket. "I'm wearing my best clothes. Besides, everybody loves a parade." He waved his battered hat to an imaginary cheering crowd.

"Look here," he went on, stopping in front of an elegant wrought-iron gate. "I'm sure the people in this magnificent house would enjoy a concert."

Beyond the gate the little group could see a big white house with tall windows. Barnaby began to play a rollicking tune as the children laughed and beat time.

Inside the house, André heard them. He should have been listening to Marie, who was reading him a story, but he had heard it many times and wasn't paying attention. He wondered whether the sun was shining. Papa had said he would take André to the market on the next fine day if he was not too busy. Today felt like the right kind of day. Warm but not too warm. If only it wasn't raining.

André listened for the sound of rain. Instead he heard music. He jumped up and hurried to the window.

An accordion was playing lustily. There was a drum too, and laughter. It sounded as if the music-makers were right outside the front gate. André wished he could see them, but all he saw as he peered through the window was a grey blur. Greyness and dark shapes were all André ever saw. He was nearly blind. He could count his fingers if he held his hand close to his eyes, but from the window he could see almost nothing.

"Who is it?" he asked.

Marie came and stood behind him. "It's the juggler," she said. "He plays for pennies in the market."

"Do you know him?"

"Of course not. But I see him often. He's about twelve years old, like you, and his clothes look as if they came out of a ragbag. But he's clever and makes everyone laugh. He can juggle and do tricks and work puppets. He plays the accordion too."

"Can we go down and listen? We could give him some pennies."

"No, André. You know your parents wouldn't allow it." Marie leaned over and shut the window.

André did know. His parents wanted him to be safe, and the big white house where he had lived all his life was the only place they considered truly safe. So Marie gave André his lessons in the little sitting room and played games with him there. He ate his meals quietly with his

parents in the grand dining room. And he rested for several hours each day because everyone thought he was frail. It was a dull life and André was often restless.

Even in the house his parents didn't let him do things for himself. They laid out his clothes, combed his hair and even cut up his food for him. "You must remember," they told him, "that you are not like other people."

Sometimes he tried to argue with them. "I could go out. I can hear and I can feel. You know how I can run up and down the stairs. I never fall. I never bump into anyone. Why couldn't I do the same out in the streets?"

"You don't know the dangers, André," his father would say. "Your mother and I don't want you to get hurt."

André came away from the window thinking about this boy, this juggler. How could a boy his own age perform in the marketplace? Where did he live? What kind of boy was he?

At lunch he was still trying to imagine being able to do something that would make people give him money, when his father suddenly said, "I'm going to the market this afternoon. Would you like to come with me, André?"

André felt like shouting with excitement, but instead he kept his voice as quiet as his father's. "Yes, Papa. I'd like to."

He remembered the way to the market very well. Out the gate and down a hill, then along a busy street. But it had been many months since his father had found time for such an expedition. The rough cobblestones of the street and the jumbled noise of people walking and talking, of horses' hoofs and cart wheels, were confusing at first. André was glad to hold onto his father's arm, but he wasn't afraid. He was excited. He loved being outside, feeling the sun on his face and hearing all the sounds of market day in Quebec City.

It always surprised André how short the walk to the market actually was. It was such a different world from the quiet, elegant Delisle house. There were people yelling and roosters crowing. There was laughter and friendly arguing. There were the smells of the fruits, vegetables and animals being sold.

Everyone knew André's father. He was an important fur merchant with a large warehouse down by the river. People greeted him as he moved through the crowds at a dignified pace. Those who knew that he had a blind son looked at André with pity. But André felt no need for pity. He was having a fine time.

M. Delisle stopped in front of a stall selling goods made of silver. He took André aside and said, "Wait here for a few minutes. I want to buy some new teaspoons for your mother."

André stood quietly, listening to his father barter with the merchant. Then he heard music. It was the same cheerful music he had heard outside the gate that morning!

"Papa," he said, "can I go over and listen to the music? I can find my way."

"Of course not, André. You would surely get lost. It's just a boy juggling for pennies. You couldn't see him anyway, and the music is terrible."

But André loved the music. And now he could hear the voice of the juggler. "How many balls do you think I can juggle at a time? One ... two ... three ... *and* an onion. Toss me a potato and I'll have soup for supper tonight. Thank you, madam. Only one potato at a time, please. I don't want to overeat."

Barnaby had to concentrate to keep five objects flying through the air, but he sneaked a quick look at the crowd. Not bad, he thought. Their eyes were following his hands as he tossed the balls, the potato and the onion in the air. They had laughed at his puppets and tapped their toes to his music. Now it was time for a few tricks.

He finished with a flourish. As he was taking his bow, he noticed a well-dressed boy edging his way through the crowd. There was something a little odd in the way he moved, but he seemed to be enjoying the show.

Barnaby made sure the egg for his next trick was safely up his sleeve. Then he went and stood in front of the boy. "I don't suppose, sir," he said, "that you realize you have an egg up your nose?"

André wasn't sure the juggler was speaking to him, until he saw the shape of the boy's hand right in front of his face and felt a gentle tug on his nose. When the crowd

laughed, André grinned, although he didn't know what had happened.

Suddenly he heard his father's angry voice and felt a tight grip on his arm. "André, I told you to wait by the stall."

"But Papa, I didn't go far. And the juggler is so much fun."

"For these people perhaps, but not for us." His father pulled him away quickly, so that he stumbled over the rough stones. Still, André couldn't help asking, "Why does he do those tricks, Papa?"

"He is a beggar. He tosses balls in the air and does silly tricks so that people will give him money and food. He should be working for a living. Forget about him." And he would talk no more about the juggler.

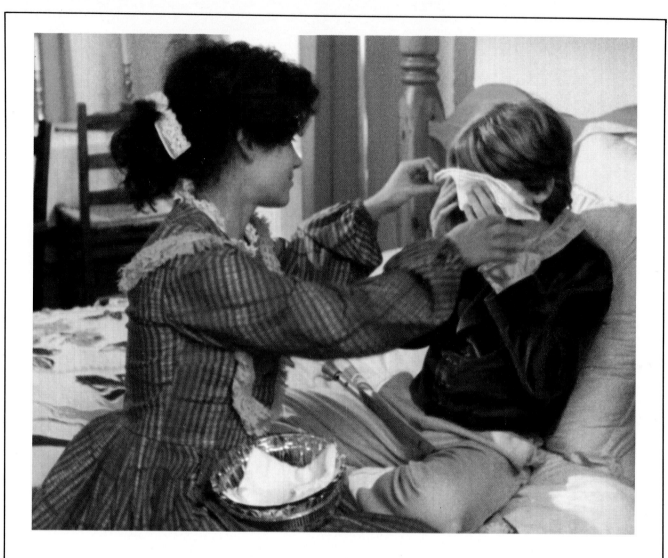

But André could not forget him. For days questions rolled around in his head. Where did the juggler live? How did he learn to do tricks? Did he really have to get food for himself? Didn't he have parents to take care of him?

One day while he was lying on his bed with compresses on his eyes, André said to himself, "The only way I'll ever know what the juggler does, and how and why, is to *ask* him. I'll go to the market and find him."

He had never before even thought of going anywhere alone. Now it seemed perfectly clear that was the only thing to do. He knew the way, he was quite sure of that. Yet his parents' warning came back to him: "You are not like other people." He heard their voices again and again. But he heard the juggler's voice too, and he had to find him.

He planned for days. He waited for a time when his mother and father would both be away from the house, and when Marie would be safely busy for several hours. Meanwhile he collected some food to take as a gift and found an old, torn shirt to wear.

Finally the day came when André found himself standing at the cellar door wearing old clothes and carrying a bundle of cakes and fruit. The door opened directly onto the street, and he was quite sure none of the servants would see him once he was out. Still, he stood with his hand on the latch for some time before he found the courage to lift it.

At last he felt the fresh air on his face. He stopped on the doorstep for a moment, getting his bearings before stepping out onto the cobblestones of the street. Just then André heard footsteps from around the corner of the house, and the gardener's angry voice: "Hey, you! Who are you? What do you think you're doing?"

For an instant André could say nothing. To be caught
before he even got away from the house! Then he realized
what the man had said. He hadn't recognized him!

"I'm an orphan," he stammered, moving cautiously
down the hill away from the gardener. "Mme Delisle gave
me food."

"Then get out, and be quick about it. Never mind
creeping along like a blind beggar."

André started to run, but stumbled and almost tripped
over some loose stones. The gardener snorted and turned
away, and André was alone in the street.

He moved slowly, feeling his way along the walls.
When he came to a crossroad and his hand felt empty air
instead of the warm, rough stone of the houses, he was
frightened. He had taken the route a dozen times in his
mind. It had seemed so clear. Now he couldn't picture it at
all.

He stood still, remembering to lean against the corner of the wall as if he were resting. In a moment his panic subsided and he began to hear the sounds around him: the rumble of cart wheels and the clop of horses' hoofs moving along the street in front of him. And voices too. People and horses and carts, all going in the same direction. This must be the street that led to the market.

André turned and with growing confidence made his way along the busy street. He could hear a babel of voices and sounds getting closer and closer. That was surely the market. But there was no music. Maybe the juggler wasn't there. He had been foolish to think he would find the boy there just any day. Perhaps he travelled from town to town. As André began to move faster, he bumped into people, who looked at him curiously.

Then he heard the music, the same tune he had heard before, and the juggler's voice. "Ladies and gentlemen, get ready for the amazing, the incredible *triple flip*!" André stopped at the edge of the crowd. When they started clapping he joined in, then waited to hear what the juggler would do next.

"And now, ladies and gentlemen, I will perform one of my most amazing tricks. I will make half of you disappear! Let me introduce my hungry hat! Don't worry, it won't eat *you*, but it does love money. Or jewellery, or gold!" The people laughed but no one moved away and André heard the sound of coins being dropped into the hat.

"What?" cried the juggler. "You're still here? My trick fails again! Well, I never liked that one much anyway. Thank you, ladies and gentlemen. I hope I'll have the pleasure of entertaining you again another day."

Now, thought André, now's the time to speak to him. He took a few steps toward the juggler, but suddenly stopped. He couldn't remember what he wanted to say. All his questions were gone.

Shyly he held out his bundle. "I brought a few things for you," he said. "I liked your show very much." Then he turned and began feeling his way toward the street that would take him home.

Barnaby took the bag and opened it to see what was inside. When he looked up, he saw the boy moving hesitantly across the marketplace. He ran after him. André heard his footsteps and turned.

Barnaby stared at him. "You were here the other day," he said. "I remember you. Only you were dressed differently."

"Yes," said André. "I wore these clothes today so I could sneak out of the house. My name is André. André Delisle."

"Is your father the fur trader? I didn't know he had a son."

André remembered how his father had dragged him away from the juggler's performance and said quickly, "What's your name? Who's your father?"

"I'm Barnaby the juggler and I don't have a father, or a mother."

"Then where do you live and who looks after you?"

"I look after myself. I ran away from the orphanage and now I live in an old stable. It's a hundred times better than the orphanage."

André was amazed. Here was someone no older than he was who could earn his own living and take care of himself.

Barnaby was watching André closely. There was something about this boy that puzzled him. "Do you want to see where I live?" he asked. "It's not far from here."

André didn't hesitate. He was already in trouble if his parents had discovered he wasn't home. He'd better see Barnaby's place now, while he had the chance. "Let's go," he said.

Barnaby started off so quickly that André couldn't tell which way he'd gone. "Wait a minute," he called. "I need to hold your arm. I can't see very well." He was a little surprised that he didn't mind saying that to Barnaby. Somehow he didn't think it would matter to this boy that he wasn't like other people.

Barnaby's face lit up. "So that's it," he said. "I knew there was something unusual about you. You get around really well, don't you?"

"Well, yes," said André. "I'm not really blind, you know." And he started to tell Barnaby just how much he could see.

As they walked, it began to rain lightly. André held out his hand and tilted his face up to feel the cool drops. "I've never walked in the rain before," he said. He could feel Barnaby turn toward him in surprise. "Never just walked slowly and really felt the rain," he explained.

Barnaby nodded. They turned into a narrow lane and he stopped at a plain wooden door. "Welcome to my home," he said formally, but with a grin. He opened the door and they went inside.

André stood still. The room was so different from any he was used to that he had to stop and sense it for a moment. The floor under his feet was uneven. There seemed to be no windows, but he could make out strange shapes and shadows everywhere.

He sniffed. "I can tell it's a stable," he said.

"Do you like it?" asked Barnaby.

"I like it a lot."

"How do you know? You can't see it."

"I can feel things about it. And anyway, I told you I can see a little — light and dark and things I hold close to my eyes."

"Well, good," exclaimed Barnaby. "Then I can show you all my stuff."

He helped André climb the ladder to the loft and sat him on the pile of hay he used for a bed. Then he began pulling out his treasures — puppets, hats, even a cuckoo clock.

"Where did you get all this?" André asked.

"Made them myself, or found them in garbage piles. Sometimes people give me things instead of money. If only I could have all the things rich people throw away, I would live like a king."

"If only I could learn some of your tricks, I would *feel* like a king."

"Well, you could," said Barnaby. "I could teach you."

"I can hardly see," objected André. "How could I do tricks?"

"Maybe you couldn't juggle," said Barnaby, "but there are lots of other things you could do. I've seen blind people who live by doing tricks."

André couldn't imagine what kind of tricks he might be able to do. He knew about magic from stories, and he had heard about clowns and buffoons who tumbled about and made people laugh. But what could *he* do? Still, Barnaby was so sure. And Barnaby should know.

He remembered what Barnaby had said about rich people's garbage. "I could bring some clothes and things you could use," he offered, "and maybe you could teach me one or two things."

"One or two?" said Barnaby. "One or two hundred at least. I've never had anyone to share my amazing skills with. You're the first." He leapt up and bowed to André, sweeping an imaginary cape wide with his arm.

"But why me? There must be people who could learn your tricks more easily."

"Maybe," said Barnaby. "But because you can't see, you already know some tricks of your own. Like how to feel a place. I think you'll pick up a lot of things fast. Anyway, I don't know anyone else. I used to work with my father and we travelled all the time. Then I was in the orphanage. But I couldn't stand being cooped up so I left, and I haven't had time to make any good friends yet."

He sat down beside André on the bed. "Can you come back tomorrow?"

"I don't know," André said. "I'll try, but I'll have to sneak out. There might be a chance in the afternoon when I'm supposed to be resting my eyes. Not that it does any good." He paused, thinking of the empty room where he was supposed to be napping right now. For a second his heart seemed to stop. "I'd better go home now," he added quickly. "If they miss me, I'll never get out again. Where's the ladder?"

"You can jump. It's much faster and it's fun."

But, looking down, André saw only darkness. How far down was the floor? What would he land on? "I can't," he said.

Barnaby saw from André's face how frightened he was. He imagined jumping down into darkness himself. "Turn around," he said. "I'll put your foot on the ladder."

It turned out to be surprisingly easy for André to escape, and he did, frequently. His naps were considered very important and he was never disturbed. Besides, no one would have believed he could make his way out of the house and through the streets alone. André sometimes thought that part of him must still be lying quietly in his tidy room while another part was walking carefully but confidently down the hill and along the lane to Barnaby's stable.

The things André was learning in that stable were even more surprising. As Barnaby had predicted, many tricks came easily to him. Sleight of hand he learned very quickly, and he became an expert at palming a coin or hiding an egg up his sleeve. He took great delight in stealing Barnaby's pocketknife and hiding it.

"It's a good thing I'm an honest juggler," Barnaby told him. "It would be easy to teach you to be a first-rate pickpocket."

"Why?" asked André.

"You never look at what your hands are doing, which is the first rule for picking pockets *and* for magic tricks. You seem to know by instinct where things are."

"Barnaby, you don't pick pockets, do you?"

"Not me. Jail would be even worse than the orphanage. I'd rather starve."

It took André a little longer to master the hand puppets, because Barnaby wanted to work out routines they could do together. "You don't really have to look at the puppets," he said, "but they have to look at each other. They're supposed to be talking or fighting or something."

Gradually they learned each other's timing and their puppets could fight, dance or fool around as the boys wanted them to. The planchette puppets were especially amusing. While Barnaby played the accordion, André played the harmonica and made them dance.

They enjoyed playing music together. André brought his flute to accompany Barnaby's drum, and even learned to beat the drum himself, with appropriate rolls and flourishes. He loved making so much noise.

Barnaby said, "You'd have no trouble gathering a crowd, but what would you say to them?" So he made André try again and again until he could say "Ladies and gentlemen! You are about to witness the most spectacular display of juggling, magic and music you've ever seen!" in a voice that shook the stable.

But the day Barnaby said, "Now I'll teach you to do a cartwheel," André answered, "I can't."

"You can," Barnaby insisted. "I won't let you bump into anything but the floor. The floor is your responsibility."

When André still hesitated, his friend said, "Look, I know it's hard to throw your body into space when you don't know what's there. But I won't let you crash or fall off anything. You can trust me. We're partners."

"I do trust you," said André. Barnaby and I really *are* partners, he thought. It was amazing, but it was true.

He tried a cartwheel. The first one flopped, but he tried again and again. It cost him some bumps and bruises, but he did learn to do a very good cartwheel.

Watching him learn, Barnaby had an idea. "You seem to have real talent for tumbling," he said. "Let's work out a clown routine. Two clowns are always better than one."

So they went out to the courtyard and worked on a lost-friends routine. With their backs to each other, they crossed and circled the square, peering around desperately. They fell over each other, but never looked to see what had tripped them. Then they accidentally crashed head-on in the middle of the courtyard and hugged each other joyously. André especially enjoyed going through this routine and adding new touches. His highly developed sense of where things were around him made it easier for him than it was for Barnaby.

One day the two of them were sitting on the edge of the loft talking, when André suddenly said, "There's a fly in here."

"It's too cold for flies," said Barnaby. "You must be imagining it."

"Maybe it's a flea then. Here he is! See here," exclaimed André. Barnaby stared at him.

"Look, he can do tricks," André went on. "He can do flips and double flips. He can do anything!"

"Anything?" said Barnaby.

"Yes, and if you don't believe me, he'll attack you."

"I don't believe you."

"All right, flea, attack!" ordered André. Then he began scratching himself frantically. "Not me, you fool! Him! Over there!"

Barnaby nearly fell over laughing. "You almost fooled me," he said. "I almost believed in that flea. I'll tell you what. I think we should keep it. A flea like that belongs in our act."

"What act?" asked André.

"Well, we should have an act. We should put together all our routines, including the flea, and put on a show. You're too funny to keep hidden away."

André wasn't sure he wanted to perform in front of people. Anyway, how could he? He would get caught for sure. But practising would be fun. So they began to put together a show.

"We'll have to wear make-up for our clown act," Barnaby announced one day. "I'll show you how to put it on, but once you get the feel of it you'll be able to do it for yourself."

He dug out an old broken mirror and some jars of white, red and black make-up. First he painted his own face, then he began to pinch and push André's as if it were made of clay. "Let's see," he said. "I think your nose should be *much* longer. And your chin should have a point."

At last he was satisfied with the result. Then André tried. He made the mouth too big and the eyebrows crooked, but he didn't care. Here in the stable everything was fun and that was all that mattered.

Soon the show seemed so real to André that he began to practise at home while he was supposed to be napping. One day he even tried a few cartwheels. Marie, who happened to be passing by, heard the thumping and opened the door. She looked at him in surprise as he turned quickly around and took a few steps toward her. "Really, André," she said, "sometimes I think you can see as well as anyone."

"Would you rather have me be like this?" he demanded. And he went crashing around the room, bumping into furniture.

"Of course not. It's just that you've changed lately. I guess you're growing up." Shaking her head, she went on about her work.

André was indeed changing, so fast that he was having a hard time keeping up with himself. He wished he could be with Barnaby every day, but that wasn't possible. His friend had a living to make, and the fine fall days were running out. So André waited for rainy days, days when the marketplace would be empty and Barnaby would be at the stable.

On one of those rainy days it happened. André's mother decided to surprise him with some sweets while he was resting. When she found he wasn't in his room, or anywhere else in the house, she rushed to her husband. "Phillipe, Phillipe!" she cried, "André is gone!"

André came quietly up the cellar stairs a short time later. Everything seemed the same as he hurried to his room. He had just sat down on the bed when his parents opened the door. His mother quickly hugged him, but his father was angry. "Where have you been?" he demanded.

"I just went for a walk to the marketplace. I can't stay in the house all the time. It's so boring here." He wanted to tell them about Barnaby and the things he had learned from him, but when he saw how angry and horrified they were that he had been out, he knew he couldn't.

"It's dangerous for you to be out in the streets alone, André," said his father. "You must not do it again or you'll be severely punished." And to make sure, he ordered that the cellar door and the iron gate be kept locked.

So André was back to a life of lessons, naps and meals, day after day. He thought of Barnaby all the time and dreamed of the show they would never be able to put on.

Barnaby wasn't surprised when André didn't show up at the stable for several days. He knew that sometimes he just couldn't get out. But when one rainy day after another went by, he began to worry.

Finally he went to André's house. He stood outside the big iron gate and stared at the high white walls. There wasn't a sign of life. He wondered which room André was in and what he was doing. Maybe he was sick.

The gardener came by. "What do you want?" he demanded.

"I want to see André," Barnaby said politely.

But the gardener yelled at him, "Get away from here! Get going!" So Barnaby had to leave, feeling more lonely than he had ever felt before.

The weather was turning colder. Sitting by the fire in the little sitting room, André wondered how his friend was doing. He knew that on such cold days people in the marketplace wouldn't stop to put money into Barnaby's hat. Perhaps Barnaby would be entertaining in taverns now. André had never been in a tavern, but he knew people went to them for amusement, and surely they would like Barnaby's music and tricks. Still, he worried. What if the tavern-keepers had no use for a young juggler?

One stormy day as Christmas neared, André said to his father, "Papa, I have a friend who has no place to go for Christmas. Could he spend it here with us?"

"I don't know who you are talking about, André. Everyone we know certainly has a place to spend Christmas."

"Remember the juggler? It's him. I'm sure he has no place to go."

"Absolutely not. We'll not have a beggar boy here. Don't bother me about it anymore."

André said no more, but he couldn't stop thinking about Barnaby. Winter was so long. Was he all right?

That night he had a dream about his friend. He saw him juggling and smiling as snow began to fall around him. Then he beckoned to André. Swirling snow fell more and more heavily, and Barnaby's face became sadder and sadder as they lost sight of each other. Finally he was gone.

André woke up sick at heart. At first he couldn't think why. Then the dream came back to him. Barnaby and the snow. Barnaby had wanted to tell him something, he was sure. Maybe something was wrong. He sat up in bed. He had to go to his friend.

It was still very early, and the room was dark. But André could hear the servants moving around, building up the fires. He got out of bed and pulled on his warmest clothes. Then over everything he put on the jacket he'd planned to wear in the show — it made him feel closer to Barnaby. Now he had to hurry. His parents would be up soon. He slipped quietly down the stairs to the cellar, where the door was still unlocked for the servants coming in. André didn't even bother to be careful. He knew that, whatever happened, he was going to find Barnaby.

The dream was still so strong in his mind that he was surprised to find it wasn't snowing. There was plenty of snow on the ground, though, and he had to be careful not to slip on the icy cobblestones as he hurried to the stable. Once there, he pounded on the door as hard as he could and shouted, "Barnaby, it's me! Barnaby, are you there?"

Barnaby heard André's voice, but at first he thought he was dreaming. When the banging and shouting didn't stop, he poked his head from under a pile of blankets.

"I'm here. I'm coming," he called. "What's all the noise? You're the one who's been missing," he added when he opened the door. "Did you get caught? What are you doing here so early in the morning?"

"I had to see you. Have you been working? Are you all right?"

"I'm all right, but I haven't been overeating, that's for sure. I could use a little work, as a matter of fact."

"Then let's do our show! Let's do it today!" André grabbed Barnaby by the hand and began twisting through one of their tumbling routines.

Barnaby shook himself free. "It's winter, in case you hadn't noticed. People don't stop to watch a juggler in winter."

"But if there are two of us, they'll stop. Besides, today is the first day of the Christmas market. It's a perfect day for our show — and I may never have another chance."

Barnaby turned a cartwheel from sheer happiness. "Then we'll do it," he said. "We'd better start getting ready."

*   *   *

M. and Mme Delisle were just finishing their breakfast tea when Marie rushed in. "Master André is nowhere to be found," she announced in a tearful voice.

"No doubt he's gone for another walk," said his father in a grim voice. "Send the servants to look through the streets. I'll go to the marketplace."

"I'm coming with you," said Mme Delisle.

*   *   *

André and Barnaby were having a wonderful time, and their routines were working beautifully. The market was crowded with people shopping for Christmas. Everyone was in a holiday mood, and they laughed and applauded enthusiastically and threw money in the hat. Barnaby was glad to hear the clinking of many coins.

"And now, ladies and gentlemen," he said, "I present to you an act known throughout the world — the Master of the Fleas!"

André stepped forward and began going through the flea routine he had practised so often. The crowd loved it.

Barnaby saw André's parents making their way through the throng. They looked anxious and upset and his heart sank. They would take André away and lock him in his room. Barnaby would never see him again.

André continued happily searching for his invisible flea. His parents glanced at him, but only fleetingly. M. Delisle was moving on when his wife cried, "No, wait! Look!" She pointed at André.

"It can't be," said M. Delisle. Then he heard the voice of the boy who was moving around so confidently, who was capturing the crowd with his skill. "But it is!"

André heard his father's voice. He knew it at once out of all the other voices in the marketplace. For an instant he hesitated. There was no use going on. Then he looked at the expectant faces in front of him. I might as well finish, he thought. It may be my last chance.

"It's a terrible thing to lose such a highly trained flea. Years I've spent, and now she's lost. I'll bet one of you stole her. You, there, I see you scratching. Did you steal my flea?"

Barnaby grinned. Even André's father must be enjoying this! How could he help it? And suddenly both Barnaby and André heard M. Delisle's laugh boom out over the marketplace.

They finished the show with a great flourish. The drum and flute sounded like a whole band. The puppets had never danced so well. Coins rained into the hat.

When it was over, André's parents couldn't stop hugging him. His father exclaimed, "You're an excellent comedian! And your flute never sounded like that before. How did you learn to do so many clever things?"

"It was Barnaby," said André. "He taught me."

So M. Delisle himself invited Barnaby for Christmas dinner. He said he wanted to ask him some questions about the juggling trade. Barnaby was delighted. He would have a warm Christmas Day, a good dinner and fun with André.

But when André led him into the grand dining room of the Delisle house on Christmas Day, Barnaby, for once in his life, was speechless. He had never seen so many candles. Everything shone — the silver, the crystal, the china. And even more, he had never seen such food!

It wasn't until he was well into his first heaping plateful of ham, turkey, potatoes and squash that he began to take part in the conversation. Soon he was telling them all about being a juggler, and about his father and mother, things he hadn't even told André. M. Delisle listened and watched. Barnaby was not what he had expected.

Soon the two boys were putting on a funny show with their puppets. That elegant room had never heard so much merrymaking. André laughed and talked as he never had before. And through the whole meal he had cut up his own food and salted it, and had passed dishes when someone asked for them. M. Delisle could see how much his son had changed.

"Would you like some more pie, Barnaby?" André asked. Barnaby groaned.

"Well, if you can't eat it today, there will be plenty left for tomorrow," M. Delisle said calmly.

Tomorrow. That was the only word André and Barnaby heard. They turned to each other and grinned. There was so much they could do tomorrow!

About the film

This book tells a story which was first told in the film *The Juggler*. How the film was made is another story.

Ariadne Ochrymovych, a Canadian producer-director, wanted to make a film that would give children some of the magic and adventure of fairy tales and legends. An old French tale about a juggler intrigued her. What if the story were about a boy who juggled in the streets of old Quebec? Or perhaps about two boys?

She talked to Michael Glassbourg, a scriptwriter, and he thought about the two characters. Barnaby could be a skilfull street performer. But his friend André should be quite different — perhaps he could be blind. The story began to develop and Michael wrote a screenplay.

The Canadian Broadcasting Corporation agreed to support the film and Ariadne was ready to look for all the other people who would be needed to make it happen. Because it would be made in Quebec, she asked Dani Hausmann of Montreal to be the associate producer, and he set about finding actors. It was especially important to find the right boys to play André and Barnaby.

Marc-André Cyr was quickly chosen to play André. Although he had never been in a film before, he had acted with Children's Creations in Montreal. The part of Barnaby was more difficult to cast. None of the boys who tried out seemed quite right. Then Dani saw Tommy Kircoff in a mock battle on a school playground and knew he would be the perfect Barnaby. Tommy was surprised when he was asked to try out for a film. In fact, he didn't believe it could happen to him and didn't come to the audition.

But he was tracked down, and soon Tommy found himself learning to juggle and do sleight-of-hand tricks. He could already tumble and do cartwheels, but he had to learn the other tricks and routines. Marc-André had a good deal to learn too. First of all he had to know what it's like to be nearly blind. He spent some time with children at the Montreal Institute for the Blind. For a while he wore goggles that made him nearly sightless. And he had to learn to be a clown.

The story was to take place in 1820, and it was important that every setting and every detail be right for that time. Quebec City's many historic streets and buildings were perfect for shooting the film. The city officials were very helpful and gave permission to use many historic buildings and locations.

André's house was made up of rooms and outside views of four different buildings. The outdoor scenes were shot in many places throughout the old city, and Barnaby's stable is the stable where the calèches and horses are kept. Even the horses were generous and shared their space with the film-makers.

Carol Paré, the production designer, was in charge of the search for suitable locations. She also researched the details of everyday life in 1820 so that clothes, food, tools — everything — would be right for the period.

After four months of research, planning and rehearsing were finished, the many people who were to make the film gathered in Quebec City. Frank Fontaine, who played André's father, lives there, as do many of the people who acted in or worked on the film. Peter Benison, the cameraman, was there with his technical crew, and many of the pictures in this book were taken from the film they shot. Others are photographs taken by Arne Glassbourg.

The film was shot in seven days in November. For some of the autumn scenes, there was already too much snow. It had to be cleared away and replaced with dry leaves. But the Christmas scenes needed more, and artificial snow had to be added.

Shooting the film was hard work. It was cold. The hours were long. The script demanded a lot, especially from the two boys, who were new to film-making. But everyone liked the story. They wanted it to work. They especially liked working with Marc-André and Tommy, whose enthusiasm was contagious even when the work was hard.

After the shooting was finished, the film was put together in Toronto by David Leach, a film editor. Original music was composed by John Welsman. Then, at the very end, a new sound track was created with French voices, to allow French as well as English viewers to enjoy the story.

And that's how *The Juggler* came to be.